Take Two

by

Jo Cotterill

Illustrated by Yishan Li

For Heather Spilberg

With special thanks to:
Anne Bergin
Amber Claybrook
Jade Claybrook
Michelle Godfrey
Sophie Hall
Christina Lawrence
Vicky MacIntyre
Chloe Powell
Charlotte Valliant

First published in 2011 in Great Britain by
Barrington Stoke Ltd
18 Walker St, Edinburgh, EH3 7LP

www.barringtonstoke.co.uk

ISBN: 978-1-84299-874-8

Printed in China by Leo

Contents

Chapter 1
Proms and Plans

"He is so yummy," said Lily with a sigh. "The yummiest thing in the world."

"I could have him for dinner," agreed her friend Carla.

They both looked across at Max Goodwin. He was tall, with dark brown hair and brown eyes, and he was captain of the rugby team.

"Good looking *and* fit," said Lily.

"What more could a girl want?" said Carla. "And look."

She pointed to a poster on the wall which said:

END OF TERM PROM

ASK YOUR DREAM DATE NOW!

"I wish Max would ask *me* to the dance," said Lily. "But I've got no chance."

Carla smiled. "A girl can dream."

The bell rang. "I've got a flute lesson," said Lily. "See you in French."

When Lily had gone, Carla went over to Max. "Hi, Max," she said. "I saw the match on Saturday. You were really cool."

"Thanks," said Max. "It was a great match."

"We only won because of you," said Carla. "That run you made was awesome."

Max rubbed his hand in his hair. "You like rugby?"

"Oh, yes," said Carla. "I wish girls could play it. I'd play scrum half."

Max laughed. "You don't look very strong."

Carla made her hand into a fist. "Feel my arm," she said. "I've got muscles."

Max laughed again. "You're so funny," he said. "Hey, do you want to go to the prom with me?'

Carla was thrilled. "I would love to!"

"Cool," said Max. "But can I ask you something? Don't tell anyone you're going with me."

Carla was puzzled. "Why not?"

Max looked around to see if anyone was near. "Lots of girls want to go with me," he said in a low voice. "It's because I'm so popular. If they know I've asked you – well, you might get some trouble."

"You're so sweet to think of me," said Carla. "Of course I won't tell anyone."

Chapter 2
Secrets and Lies

At the end of school, Lily was trying to put her books in her locker. "Not again!" she said, as they fell on to the floor.

"Here." Max picked them up for her.

"Oh!" Lily blushed. "Thank you."

"It's Lily, isn't it?" said Max. He leaned

on her locker. "You're in my Maths class."

Lily didn't know where to look. Max

Goodwin was talking to her! "Yes," she said.

"Is it you who plays the flute?" said Max. "Were you playing this morning in the music room?"

"Yes," said Lily again, and blushed even more.

Max looked into her eyes. "It sounded amazing. You're really good."

"Thank you," she said and smiled.

"Wow," said Max. "You've got an amazing smile, too."

Lily almost fell over in shock! She muttered, "Oh, um, ah, do you think so?"

"I've been wanting to ask you something," said Max. "Would you go with me to the prom?"

"Me?" said Lily with a sort of squeak. "You – you're asking *me* to the prom?"

Max nodded. "But let's keep it a secret, OK?" He grinned. "Then we can surprise everyone at the dance."

Lily felt like she might faint. "All right," she said, trying to sound normal.

"Cool," said Max. "Catch you later."

****

"I've got a date for the prom!" Lily and Carla said at the same time. Then they looked at each other.

"Who's yours?" asked Lily.

Carla wagged her finger. "Not telling."

Lily frowned. "We tell each other everything."

"Not this," said Carla. She grinned. "If I tell you who it is, you'll hate me."

"I would never hate you," said Lily. "You're my friend."

"Still not telling," said Carla.

Lily felt cross. "Fine. Then I'm not telling you who *my* date is. Just you wait!"

Chapter 3
Truth and Ideas

Lily was out shopping. She wanted to buy a blue prom dress because Max liked blue.

"What about this one?" asked the lady in the shop.

Lily shook her head. "No." She looked around. Hanging on the wall behind the pay desk was a beautiful blue dress with sparkles. "Can I try that one?"

"Sorry," said a voice. "That's mine."

Lily turned. "Carla!"

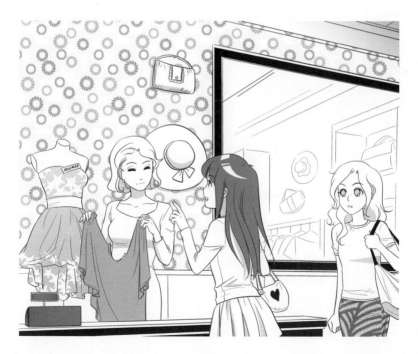

"Lily! I didn't see you. You buying a dress too?"

Lily nodded. "Not found anything I like yet, apart from that one."

"Sorry," said Carla. "I tried it on yesterday. It fits like a glove. And it's blue too."

Lily looked at her. "What do you mean?"

"My date likes blue," said Carla. "It's his favourite colour."

Lily frowned. "That's odd."

Carla laughed. "You are funny, Lily. Why is it odd?"

"My date likes blue too," said Lily.

Carla gave a shrug. "Lots of people like blue."

"Yes, but ..." Lily took a deep breath. "Carla, will you tell me who you're going with? Cross my heart I won't tell anyone."

"No, it's a secret," said Carla.

"I'll tell you mine," said Lily. "Please, Carla. I've got a funny feeling about this."

"You're being so weird today, Lily," said Carla. She gave a sigh. "Oh, all right. Tell me who *you're* going with."

Lily bit her lip. "Max Goodwin."

Carla's mouth fell open. "*Who?*"

"Max Goodwin."

"But – but you can't be!" spluttered Carla. "*I'm going with Max Goodwin!*"

"What a rat," said Carla when they were back at Lily's house. "Asking us *both* to the prom."

"How many girls has he asked, do you think?" said Lily.

Carla looked cross. "I don't know. But it's a mean thing to do. We could have stopped being friends over this."

"Maybe that's what he wants," said Lily. "Girls fighting over him."

"That's horrid," said Carla. "We should tell him we've found out. In front of everyone."

"In front of everyone?" said Lily. Her eyes started to shine. "I've just had an even better idea, Carla. Let's *both* go with him to the prom!"

Carla looked shocked. "What?"

"Yes!" said Lily. "Don't you see? It's the best way to get back at him! This is what we're going to do ..."

Chapter 4
Fun and Flirting

Max rubbed his hands in his hair to make it look messy. He loved it when girls followed him around. It gave him a sense of power. And he had *two* dates for the prom! He grinned as he thought about Lily and Carla. They wouldn't like having to share a boy. They would fight over him at the prom

– that would show everyone how popular he was!

"Max!" Carla ran up to him. "I'm so glad to see you! I've got my dress and everything."

"Cool," said Max. "You looking forward to it then?"

"Oh, yes," said Carla, and she giggled. "I can't wait! I love dancing! And I get to spend the whole evening with *you*."

"Yeah," said Max. "That is pretty cool. Most girls would kill for that."

Carla wanted to laugh. Didn't Max know how silly he was?

"So, Carly ..." said Max.

"Carla."

"Yeah. You haven't told anyone else, have you?"

Carla opened her eyes very wide. "Oh, *no*! I don't want the other girls to feel bad that you didn't ask them. I haven't told *anyone*!" She crossed her fingers behind her back.

"Cool," said Max. "Well, see you later."

Around the corner, Max met Lily. "Hey, Lily," he said. "You excited about the prom?"

Lily smiled. "Of course! I can't wait! I'm so thrilled that you asked me!"

"Yeah," said Max. "I can see why that makes you happy. You're a lucky girl."

Lily wanted to burst out laughing but she held it in and said, "I know, Max. You're the most popular boy in school."

"That's true," said Max. He rubbed his hand in his hair again. "You haven't told anyone about us, have you?"

Lily smiled. "I can keep a secret, Max."

"Cool. Well, see you later."

"Oh, Max!" Lily called.

"Yeah?"

Lily smiled her sweetest smile. "You're getting me flowers, right?"

Max was puzzled. "Flowers?"

"Yes. The boy always gets the girl flowers," said Lily. "Didn't you know?"

"Oh," said Max. "Flowers. Yeah. OK."

Later Lily met up with Carla.

"I told Max he had to buy me flowers," said Lily with a giggle. "That boys always do."

"He'll have to get flowers for both of us then," said Carla. She grinned. "It will cost twice as much! Good thinking, Lily!"

"'Well," said Lily, "he's too up himself. I was nearly sick, all that stuff he said about being so popular."

"Me too," said Carla. "What did we ever see in him?"

"Come round to my house before the prom," said Lily. "We'll get ready together."

"And turn up together," said Carla. "Max won't know what's hit him!"

Chapter 5
Dance and Dazzle

It was the day of the dance, and the two girls were round at Lily's house.

"You look amazing," said Lily to Carla. "I'm so glad you got that dress. It suits you really well."

Carla did a twirl and her skirt flew out at the sides. It was a perfect fit. "Thanks, Lily," she said. "You look nice too."

"Thanks." Lily was pleased. Her dress was dark blue with little sparkles on it. It reached nearly down to the floor, with a low back. She looked very elegant.

"The flowers came this afternoon," said Carla with a grin. "They must have cost a lot."

"Mine too," said Lily. "I still can't believe Max sent us the same ones. We both have white roses! What a dork!"

Carla grinned. "You ready? It's time to go!"

Max was waiting outside the school hall. "Carla, hi!" Then he saw Lily behind her. "And – uh – hi, Lily!"

"Hi, Max!" said Carla. "I hope you don't mind. I told Lily I was going with you."

"And I said that's funny because I was going with you too!" said Lily.

"Yeah," said Max. "Sorry about that." He didn't look sorry.

"Let's go in," said Carla. "I want to dance!"

Max was puzzled. He looked at Lily and then at Carla. Why weren't they mad at each other?

"Come on," said Lily, linking her arm with his. "This is going to be such a good night!"

Max took a breath. Then he smiled. Everyone would still admire him. He had two pretty girls with him! "Let's go," he said. Maybe once the girls knew they had to share him, they would get cross with each other?

Lily and Carla winked at each other behind Max's back. Now for the next part of the plan!

Chapter 6
Take Two and Party!

Inside, the school hall was full of gold and silver balloons. A band was playing on the stage. "Wow!" said Carla. "This looks great!"

Lily was skipping up and down. "I love this song! Come on, Max, let's dance!" The two girls dragged him on to the dance floor.

"Oh, no," Max said with a laugh. "I can't dance with *both* of you at the same time." He looked hopeful. Would they fight over who could dance with him first?

Carla gave a shrug. "OK. Lily, you have the first dance. I'll get a drink."

"OK!" said Lily.

Max frowned. This was a bit odd. But maybe if he got up close to Lily, and Carla saw it ...

"Hey!" said Lily as Max grabbed her round the waist. "I can't dance if you're that close!" She pushed him away with a laugh.

When the song ended and the next one began, Carla came back. She was smiling. "My turn!"

"Watch him," said Lily with a wink. "He's trying to get a bit too close." She punched Max on the arm in a playful way. "Keep your hands to yourself, rugby captain!"

Max didn't know what was going on. Didn't these girls fancy him? They must do! Maybe Lily wouldn't like it if he kissed Carla ...

Max waited until Lily was coming back. Then he pulled Carla close and kissed her. That would make Lily mad, wouldn't it?

But Lily just laughed. "You two!" she said. "That's very naughty! If the teachers see you, you'll get into trouble!"

Carla grinned. "Hey, I was just trying him out for you."

Lily joined Max on the dance floor as Carla went to sit down. "I love dancing with you!" she said.

Max was getting a strange sinking feeling. This wasn't working out the way he'd hoped. "I need to sit down," he said.

"Oh, no," said Lily. "It's my turn. You said you could only dance with one of us at a time. So you owe me a dance." She grabbed his hands. "Dance with me!"

Carla and Lily made Max dance to all of the songs. They didn't let him sit down once. "I need a drink," said Max. He was feeling very hot.

44

"I'll get you one," said Carla. But she came back without it.

"Where's my drink?" asked Max.

"Oh, sorry!" said Carla. "I forgot."

"I'll get one," said Max, but Carla grabbed his arm.

"You can't go now, it's my turn to dance with you!"

Max tried one last time. "The girl who likes me most can get me a drink," he said.

But the two girls just giggled. "You're so silly!" said Lily. "We both like you the same!" *Which is true*, she thought to herself. *We don't like him at all!*

By eleven pm, Max was very tired indeed. "I need to sit down!" he moaned.

"But it's the last song!" said Lily.

"I don't care!" said Max. "You two are driving me mad!"

Chapter 7
Shout and Shame!

Carla and Lily looked at each other. "Good!" they said at the same time. "It serves you right," added Carla.

Max wiped his face on his sleeve. "What are you talking about?"

Carla put her hands on her hips. "Did you think it was funny to ask two girls to the same prom?" she said. One or two people dancing close by looked up.

"Yeah," said Lily, in a loud voice. "Did you *really* think we would be OK about it?"

"Er ..." said Max.

"Did you want us to fight over you?" asked Carla.

Max tried to laugh. "Why would you think that?"

Lily said, "All night you've been trying to make us argue over you."

"Treating us like we had to fight to win you!" said Carla. She looked cross. "We're best friends, Lily and me. Did you really think we would break up our friendship over you?"

"Just to make you look good," added Lily, her face pink with anger.

"You didn't seem to mind," Max said. The girls were talking in very loud voices now. He hoped other people didn't hear.

"Only because we knew what you were up to," said Carla in disgust. "You complete loser!"

"Me? A loser?" said Max. That made him angry. "I'm the captain of the rugby team. Every girl wants to go out with me!"

"Well here are two girls who *don't*!" said Carla. "Me and Lily!"

"And me," said a girl's voice. Max turned round to see a whole crowd of people watching. "What an idiot!" he heard one of them say.

"I wouldn't go out with Max if you paid me," said another girl. "He's so full of himself!"

"But look at him now," said one of the boys. "Out-witted by two girls!"

The people in the crowd started to laugh.

"Max Goodwin, Most Popular Boy!" jeered
one.

"Nice tactics, Captain!" shouted another.

Max felt his face get even hotter. He didn't like people making fun of him. His hair was stuck to his head with gel and sweat, and his face was pink with shame.

"I don't think he'll ever ask two girls to the same dance again," Lily said.

"I don't think he'd find two girls who would say yes!" said Carla.

They looked at each other and grinned.

"Come on, Carla," said Lily. "I think it's time we left."

Carla nodded. "Job done."

They turned and marched out.

Behind them, people started clapping and cheering. Max looked like he wanted to run away.

Carla and Lily laughed all the way home. "That'll teach him!" said Carla.

"Oh, Carla," said Lily. "Let's never fancy the same boy again. It's too much trouble."

"Deal," said Carla. "So I hope you don't like Peter Grant. He's my new crush."

"Peter Grant?" said Lily. "Oh, no, you can't have him. He's so cute!"

They looked at each other.

And then they burst into giggles again.